YOU ARE INCREDIBLY PERFECT

POETRY FOR LONELY HEARTS, FINDING HOME IN WORDS

AVISHKA SINGH

a ishya

Contents

Contents

Contents

Foreword

In the tapestry of friendship, woven with threads of shared experiences and cherished moments, there are those rare individuals who leave an indelible mark on our lives. Avishka is one such soul—a beacon of light amidst life's myriad shades, a poet whose words resonate with the beauty and complexity of the human spirit. As I pen these words, I am humbled to have the opportunity to introduce you to Avishka's exquisite collection of poems, "You Are Incredibly Perfect." Within these pages, you will discover a world where emotions flow like rivers, where dreams take flight on the wings of imagination, and where every word is a testament to the power of the human heart. Avishka's poetry is a symphony of vulnerability and strength, of fragility and resilience. With each verse, she invites you to journey deep within yourself, to explore the depths of your own soul and embrace the fullness of your being. Her words are not just reflections of her own experiences but mirrors that reveal the shared humanity that binds us all.

"You Are Incredibly Perfect" is more than a book of poetry; it is a tribute to the beauty found in imperfection, a celebration of the uniqueness that defines us as individuals. As you immerse yourself in Avishka's world, may you find solace in the knowledge that you are not alone, that your joys and sorrows are echoed in the verses of countless others. So, dear reader, let these poems be your guiding stars, lighting the way through life's darkest moments and illuminating the path to self-discovery. And may you, like Avishka, embrace the truth that perfection is not found in flawlessness but in the courage to be authentically, incredibly, perfectly, you.

— *Aditya*

Preface

As I sit down to write this preface for my first poetry collection, you are incredibly perfect," Poetry for Lonely Hearts, Finding Home in Words"

I find myself reflecting on the journey that has led me to this moment. At the age of 18, I am embarking on a new chapter of creative expression, eager to share my thoughts and emotions through the art of poetry. This collection is a testament to my personal exploration of self-love and the quest for understanding reality. Through these poems, I seek to capture the raw and authentic experiences of navigating life as a young adult—embracing vulnerabilities, celebrating strengths, and confronting truths. Poetry has been my sanctuary—a place where I can weave words into emotions and thoughts, allowing me to make sense of the complexities of existence. Each poem within this collection reflects my inner world, shaped by my experiences, observations, and aspirations. I hope that as you delve into these pages, you find resonance and connection with the themes explored here. Whether you are also on a journey of self-discovery or simply seeking moments of introspection, my hope is that these poems offer solace, inspiration, and perhaps even a newfound perspective. I am immensely grateful for the opportunity to share my poetry with you, dear reader. Your presence here makes this endeavour all the more meaningful. As I continue to grow and evolve as a writer, I invite you to join me on this creative odyssey.

Thank you for embarking on this poetic adventure with me.

Warm regards,

Avishka Singh

Acknowledgements

"I would like to express my heartfelt gratitude to the many individuals who have contributed to the creation and realization of this poetry collection, you are incredibly perfect," Poetry for Lonely Hearts, Finding Home in Words". "

First and foremost, my deepest thanks go to my family and friends for their unwavering support, encouragement, and belief in my creative endeavours. Your love and understanding have sustained me throughout this journey of self-discovery and expression. I am incredibly grateful to my mentors and fellow poets whose guidance, wisdom, and feedback have played a crucial role in shaping the themes and sentiments explored within these verses. Your insights and encouragement have enriched this collection in profound ways. I extend special thanks to the readers who resonate with the emotions and experiences captured in these poems. Your engagement and connection with the words on these pages give purpose and meaning to my work as a poet. I must also acknowledge the broader community of artists, thinkers, and seekers whose collective creativity and passion for self-expression continuously inspire and motivate me. Lastly, I wish to express my gratitude to the universe itself—the wellspring of endless mysteries and revelations. May the light of understanding and self-acceptance shine through these poems and touch the hearts of those who journey through these verses. This book is a testament to the transformative power of self-love and the courage to confront reality with open eyes and an open heart. Thank you all for being part of this profound exploration.

With heartfelt appreciation

Avishka Singh

Prose And Poetry About

loving

learning

leaving

hoping

healing

hurting

growing

believing

blooming

empathy

reflection

acceptance

in no specific order

Reciprocity

Don't beg, don't force, don't chase, give the same energy they gave

In the dance of give and take,

Let reciprocity be our guide,

A balance sought for its own sake,

Where equal measures do reside.

No need to beg or force or chase,

For energy flows where it's embraced,

In harmony, a gentle grace,

Where mutual respect is traced.

If they give love, then love they'll find, If kindness is their chosen
line,

In echoes of the heart and mind,

A symphony of souls entwined.

So let us offer what's been lent,

And in return, our hearts content,

For in this cycle, love is sent.

A bond that's true and never spent.

<u>**Reciprocity**</u>

Reciprocity is the melody of life's symphony,

where giving and receiving dance in harmony,

echoing the beauty of mutual respect and understanding.

1. Tough Love

The golden thread of a highly successful and meaningful life is self – discipline. Discipline allows you to do all those things you know in your heart you should do but never feel like doing. Without self – discipline, you will not set clear goals, manage your time effectively, treat people well, persist through the tough times, care for your health or think positive thoughts. I call the habit of self – discipline "Tough Love" because getting tough with yourself is actually a very loving gesture. By being stricter with yourself, you will begin to live life more deliberately, on your own terms rather than simply reacting to life the way a leaf floating in a stream drifts according to the flow of the current on a particular day. The tougher you are on yourself, the easier life will be on you. The quality of your life ultimately is shaped by the quality of your choices and decisions, ones that range from the career you choose to pursue to the books you read, the time that you wake up every morning and the thoughts you think during the hours of your days, when you consistently flex your willpower by making those choices that you know are the right ones (rather than the easy ones), you take back control of your life. Effective, fulfilled people do not spend their time doing what is most convenient and comfortable. They have the courage to listen to their hearts and to do the wise thing. This habit is what makes them great. "The successful person has the habit of doing the things failures don't like to do,"Perhaps the most valuable result of all education is the ability to make yourself do the thing you have to do, when it ought to be done, whether you like it or not. Whatever we learn to do, we learn by actually doing it: men come to be builders, for instance, by building, and harp players, by playing the harp. In the same way, by doing just acts we come to be just; by doing self – controlled acts, we come to be self – controlled; and by doing brave acts, we come to be brave.

2. Honor Your Past

Every second you dwell on the past you steal from your future. Every minute you spend focusing on your problems you take away from finding your solutions. And thinking about all those things that you wish never happened to you is actually blocking all the things you want to happen from entering into your life. Given the timeless truth that hold that you become what you think about all day long, it makes no sense to worry about past events or mistakes unless you want to experience them for a second time. Instead, use the lessons you have learned from your past to rise to a whole new level of awareness and enlightenment. Life's greatest setbacks reveal life's biggest opportunities. As the ancient thinker Euripides noted, "There is in the worst of fortune the best chances for a happy change." If you have suffered more than your fair share of difficulties in life, perhaps you are being prepared to serve some greater purpose that will require you to be equipped with the wisdom you have acquired through your trials. Use these life lessons to fuel your future growth. Remember, happy people have often experienced as much adversity as those who are unhappy. What sets them apart is that they have the good sense to manage their memories in a way that enriches their lives. And understand that if you have failed more than others, there is a very good chance you are living more completely than others. Those who take more chances and dare to be more and do more than others will naturally experience more failures. But personally, I would rather have the bravery to try something and then fail than never to have tried it at all. I would much prefer spending the rest of my days expanding my human frontiers and trying to make the seemingly impossible probable than live a life of comfort, security and mediocrity. That's the essence of true life success. Booker T. Washington said, "I have learned that success is to be measured not so much by the position that one has reached in life as by the obstacles he has overcome while trying to succeed."

Echoes of Honor

In the vaults of memory, where shadows dance,

Like the echoes of moments, steeped in chance.

The heroes of yore, in their silent home.

Their valorous acts, like stars in the night,

Illuminate the path with guiding light.

With sword and shield, they stood side by side,

In battle's fury, they did not hide.

Their courage, a beacon for all to see,

A legacy of honor, eternally free.

Though the sands of time may shift and change,

Their spirit endures, steadfast and strange.

For in their deeds, a sacred flame does burn,

A testament to the glory they earned.

So let us raise our voices high,

And sing of their deeds to the endless sky.

For though they may be gone from sight,

Their memory shines forever bright.

A tapestry woven with threads of time,

Each stitch is a testament to sublime deeds.

Through the corridors of history they roam,

The heroes of yore, in their silent home.

Their valorous acts, like stars in the night,

Illuminate the path with guiding light.

With sword and shield, they stood side by side, in battle's fury,
they did not hide. Their courage, a beacon for all to see,

A legacy of honor, eternally free.

Though the sands of time may shift and change,

their spirit endures, steadfast and strange.

For in their deeds, a sacred flame does burn,

A testament to the glory they did earn.

So let us raise our voices high

and sing of their deeds to the endless sky.

For though they may be gone from sight,

Their memory shines forever bright.

3. Reawakening the Inner Child

You can understand and relate the most people better if you look at them – no matter how impressive they may be – as if they are children. For most of us never really grow up or mature all that much – we simply grow taller. Oh, to be sure, we laugh less and play less and wear uncomfortable disguises like adults, but beneath the costume is the child we always are, whose needs are simple, whose daily life is still best described by fairy tales.

To the inner child,

I'm sorry you never learned how the words are,'I'm proud of you' were supposed to feel. I'm sorry you never had a shoulder to lean on. I'm sorry you felt alone. I'm sorry you were never told you're enough. I'm sorry I never told you how much I love you. The child is still & sometimes not so still.

It is waiting for a genuine, heartfelt apology.

4. Nature's Embrace: A Path to Healing

During teenage years, the heart can often feel aloof, distant, and burdened by a heavy cloak of loneliness. It's a time when the world can seem vast and indifferent, leaving young souls to navigate the labyrinth of emotions on their own. But amidst this solitude, there lies a beacon of hope, a pathway to healing that often goes unnoticed—the gentle embrace of nature. I remember those days all too well. Feeling adrift in a sea of uncertainty, my heart weighed down by the weight of unspoken words and unshed tears. It was as if I were an island unto myself, separated from the world by an invisible barrier of isolation. But little did I know that the cure for my loneliness lay just beyond my doorstep, waiting patiently for me to discover its healing touch. Nature has a remarkable way of soothing the soul, of whispering secrets of solace to those who are willing to listen. It doesn't demand explanations or offer judgment; it simply exists, a sanctuary of serenity in a chaotic world. For me, it was the rustle of leaves in the gentle breeze, the symphony of birdsong at dawn, and the soft caress of sunlight filtering through the branches. In the arms of nature, I found refuge from the storm raging within me—a safe haven where I could shed my armor and be vulnerable, unafraid of rejection or ridicule. As I immersed myself in the natural world, something miraculous began to happen. The walls around my heart started to crumble, replaced by a sense of connectedness and belonging that I had long yearned for. I realized that I was not alone—that I was part of something much greater than myself, woven into the intricate tapestry of life that surrounds us all. And in that realization, I found healing. But nature's healing touch is not confined to the physical realm; it extends deep into the recesses of the soul, offering solace to even the most wounded hearts. It teaches us patience and resilience, reminding us that just as the seasons ebb and flow, so too do our own trials and tribulations. It shows us the beauty of impermanence, urging us to embrace change rather than fear it. And above all, it instills within us a sense of wonder and gratitude for the precious gift of life itself.

So to those teenage hearts who feel aloof and adrift, know that you are not alone. Turn to nature with an open mind and an open heart and let its healing embrace wash over you like a gentle tide. For in the quietude of the natural world, you may just find the answers you seek—the solace you crave, and the healing you deserve.

5. Overcoming Envy, Jealousy, and Disappointment

As the writer of this exploration into the complexities of human emotions, I invite you to embark on a journey with me – a journey to understand and ultimately overcome the powerful trio of envy, jealousy, and disappointment. These emotions, though deeply ingrained in human experience, have the potential to hinder our happiness and rob us of our inner peace. But fear not, for through introspection and self-awareness, we can navigate these turbulent waters and emerge stronger and more resilient than ever before.

Envy, that gnawing feeling that arises when we perceive others to possess something we desire, can consume us if left unchecked. We look upon the lives of others with longing, convinced that their success, their relationships, their possessions hold the key to our own happiness. But the truth is, envy blinds us to the abundance that already exists in our own lives. It distorts our perception of reality, convincing us that we are lacking in comparison to others. Yet, if we shift our focus from what we lack to what we have, we can cultivate gratitude and appreciation for the blessings that surround us.

Jealousy, a close cousin of envy, rears its ugly head when we feel threatened by the success or achievements of others. It stems from a place of insecurity and fear – a fear of being replaced, overlooked, or deemed unworthy. But jealousy, like all emotions, is a product of our own inner turmoil. It speaks volumes about our own insecurities and inadequacies rather than the accomplishments of others. By acknowledging and addressing these underlying issues, we can liberate ourselves from the shackles of jealousy and celebrate the successes of others as a testament to the infinite possibilities that exist within each of us.

Disappointment, perhaps the most universal of human emotions, arises when our expectations fail to align with reality. We invest our hopes and dreams in a particular outcome, only to be met with disappointment when things don't go as planned. But disappointment, far from being a sign of failure, is an opportunity for growth and self-discovery. It teaches us resilience, humility, and the importance of adaptability in the face of adversity. By reframing our perspective and embracing life's inevitable twists and turns, we can transform disappointment into an opportunity for personal evolution and empowerment.

As the writer of your own narrative, I encourage you to embrace these emotions as valuable teachers on the journey to self-awareness and inner peace. Rather than allowing envy, jealousy, and disappointment to control your thoughts and actions, choose instead to confront them with courage and compassion. Seek understanding in moments of conflict, find solace in moments of adversity, and celebrate the inherent beauty of the human experience in all its messy, imperfect glory. For it is through the acceptance and transcendence of these emotions that we unlock the door to true happiness and fulfillment.

6. The Crucible of Transformation

In the journey towards the life we yearn for, there stands a formidable obstacle, a mountain blocking our path. This mountain represents the barriers between us and the fulfillment we seek. Yet, paradoxically, it also holds the key to our liberation and evolution. It is at the foot of this mountain, where the flames of adversity burn hottest, that we find ourselves confronted with a pivotal moment.

It is often a trigger—a wound laid bare—that propels us to this precipice. This wound, raw and achingly real, serves as a compass, guiding us towards our true purpose. In facing it, we begin to discern the faint outlines of our destined path. But first, we must traverse the treacherous terrain of our own inner landscape. At this juncture, we are at the crux of a profound breakdown. Yet, within this crucible of chaos lies the potential for breakthrough. Our old selves, once stalwart companions on the journey thus far, are now burdened by the weight of our burgeoning aspirations. It is time to bid them farewell, to release them into the consuming flames of our vision. In mourning the loss of our former selves, we make space for the emergence of something new, something yet untested and unfamiliar. We must dare to venture into uncharted territory, to conceive of possibilities beyond the confines of our past experiences.

To embrace this metamorphosis, we must cultivate agility, resilience, and self-understanding. We must be willing to shed our old skins entirely, to undergo a transformation so profound that we emerge irrevocably changed. This task is both silent and monumental, a silent pact made with oneself to embark on a journey of radical self-reinvention. It is a feat that few dare to attempt, yet for those courageous enough to venture forth, it holds the promise of profound metamorphosis. As we stand at the threshold of this new beginning, we must envision ourselves not as we are, but as we aspire to be. We must become the architects of our own destiny, the heroes of our own narrative, forging a path towards a future brimming with possibility and purpose. The road ahead is fraught with uncertainty, yet within that uncertainty lies the seeds of our own potential. It is a journey that will demand our unwavering commitment, our unyielding resolve, and our steadfast belief in the transformative power of the human spirit.

Whispers of the Sea: A Journey to Self-Love

Embrace yourself like water embraces the shore, with gentle waves of acceptance Eand soothing currents of self-love.

7. The Power of Belief

In the vast expanse of human potential, belief stands as a beacon, illuminating the path to our deepest desires and loftiest aspirations. It is the cornerstone upon which dreams are built and the catalyst for transformative change. In this chapter, we delve into the profound influence of belief and its role in shaping our reality. Belief is the silent force that propels us forward, even in the face of uncertainty and adversity. It is the unwavering conviction that we are capable of achieving greatness, regardless of the obstacles that may stand in our way. Like a seed planted in fertile soil, belief germinates within the depths of our consciousness, taking root and blossoming into action. Yet, belief is more than mere optimism or wishful thinking; it is a fundamental shift in perspective, a reorientation of the mind towards possibility and potential. When we believe in ourselves and our abilities, we unlock a reservoir of inner strength and resilience that empowers us to overcome any challenge. But belief extends beyond the confines of the self; it permeates every aspect of our lives, shaping our relationships, our careers, and our sense of purpose. When we believe in the inherent goodness of others, we foster connections built on trust and mutual respect. When we believe in the possibility of a brighter future, we become architects of change, striving to leave a lasting impact on the world around us.

Yet, belief is not without its trials. Doubt and skepticism may cloud our vision, casting shadows of uncertainty upon our path. In these moments, it is essential to cultivate a sense of faith—faith in ourselves, faith in others, and faith in the inherent order of the universe. For it is through faith that we find the courage to persevere, to press onward in pursuit of our dreams, even when the road ahead seems daunting. In the end, belief is a choice—a choice to embrace the inherent potential within ourselves and the world around us. It is a choice to see beyond the limitations of the present moment and to envision a future brimming with possibility and promise. And though the journey may be fraught with challenges and setbacks, we embark upon it with a steadfast belief in the power of the human spirit to transcend, to transform, and to thrive.

8. Embracing Acceptance: The Gateway to Inner Peace

In the tapestry of human experience, acceptance serves as a golden thread, weaving through the fabric of our lives, binding together the disparate pieces of our existence. It is a journey of surrender, a profound act of acknowledging and embracing the reality of the present moment. In this chapter, we explore the transformative power of acceptance and its profound implications for our well-being. Acceptance is not passive resignation; rather, it is an active choice to make peace with the aspects of our lives that lie beyond our control. It is the recognition that resistance only serves to deepen our suffering, while acceptance liberates us from the shackles of discontent. When we embrace acceptance, we free ourselves from the burden of trying to force life to conform to our expectations, and instead, we open ourselves to the beauty of what is. At its core, acceptance is an invitation to lean into discomfort, to sit with the complexities of our emotions without judgment or resistance. It is a radical act of self-compassion, allowing us to hold space for our pain and our joy with equal tenderness. When we accept ourselves fully, flaws and all, we cultivate a deep sense of self-love that transcends the boundaries of our perceived limitations. But acceptance extends beyond the confines of the self; it permeates every facet of our relationships and interactions with the world around us. When we accept others as they are, without trying to change or fix them, we foster connections built on empathy and understanding. We create a space where authenticity can flourish, where masks can be cast aside, and where true intimacy can blossom.

Yet, acceptance is not always easy. It requires courage—the courage to face our fears, to confront our insecurities, and to embrace the inherent uncertainty of life. It requires vulnerability—the willingness to open our hearts to the full spectrum of human experience, from the depths of despair to the heights of ecstasy. And it requires humility—the recognition that we are all flawed and imperfect beings, doing the best we can with the tools we have been given. In the end, acceptance is a practice—a daily ritual of surrender and grace. It is a journey of self-discovery, a pilgrimage to the depths of our souls, where we encounter the truth of who we are and who we are meant to be. And though the path may be winding and steep, with each step we take towards acceptance, we inch closer to the elusive oasis of inner peace and contentment that resides within us all.

9. Blossoming: A Journey of Self-Discovery

In the garden of life, each soul is a delicate seed, waiting to unfurl its petals and bask in the warmth of the sun. This journey of blooming is a symphony of growth and transformation, a dance between vulnerability and resilience, as we navigate the fertile soil of our own existence. Like a flower pushing through the earth, our journey begins in darkness—a place of uncertainty and doubt. Yet, even in the depths of the soil, there lies a silent promise of possibility, a whisper of potential waiting to be realized. And so, with courage as our compass, we begin to unfurl our roots and reach towards the light. As we emerge from the shadows, we are met with the gentle caress of the breeze, the kiss of the sun upon our petals. It is here, in the tender embrace of vulnerability, that we find the courage to bloom. For it is only by opening ourselves to the world that we can fully experience the beauty of life unfolding around us. But blooming is not without its challenges. We may face storms that threaten to uproot us, winds that buffet us from every direction. Yet, it is in these moments of adversity that we discover our true strength—that resilience that lies dormant within us, waiting to be awakened. And so, with each petal that unfurls, we find ourselves transformed—rooted in the earth, yet reaching towards the heavens. We become a living testament to the power of growth and renewal, a reminder that even in the darkest of times, there is always the promise of a new beginning. But blooming is not just a solitary journey—it is a collective act of creation, a testament to the interconnectedness of all life. As we bloom, we inspire others to do the same, creating a tapestry of beauty and resilience that stretches far beyond the boundaries of our own existence. And so, let us embrace the journey of blooming with open hearts and open minds, knowing that each step we take brings us closer to the fullness of our own potential. For in the act of blooming, we discover not only who we are, but who we are meant to be—a radiant expression of the divine beauty that resides within us all.

Monochrome Majesty: The Timeless Elegance of Tulips

Like tulips in bloom, may you embrace your uniqueness with grace, for it is in the acceptance of your own colors that you truly blossom into the masterpiece you are.

10. A Journey Towards Wholeness

In the intricate mosaic of human experience, healing is a sacred thread that weaves its way through the fabric of our lives, stitching together the fragments of our brokenness into a mosaic of resilience and renewal. It is a journey of restoration, a pilgrimage to the depths of our souls, where we confront the wounds that linger beneath the surface and embark upon a path towards wholeness. Healing is not a linear process; it is a labyrinth of twists and turns, of peaks and valleys, as we navigate the landscape of our own inner terrain. It is a journey that demands courage—the courage to face our pain, to sit with our discomfort, and to embrace the vulnerability that comes with opening our hearts to the possibility of healing. Yet, healing is also a journey of empowerment—a reclaiming of agency, a rediscovery of the inherent resilience that lies within each of us. It is a journey of self-compassion, as we learn to treat ourselves with the same kindness and care that we would extend to a cherished friend. It is a journey of self-discovery, as we unearth the buried treasures of our own wisdom and strength. But healing is not just an individual endeavor; it is a collective act of compassion and solidarity. It is a recognition of the interconnectedness of all beings, a commitment to holding space for one another as we navigate the complexities of our shared humanity. It is a reminder that in our vulnerability lies our greatest strength—that it is through our wounds that we find our common humanity, our shared capacity for empathy and understanding. And so, as we embark upon the journey of healing, let us do so with open hearts and open minds, knowing that we are not alone. Let us lean on one another for support, drawing strength from the knowledge that we are all in this together. Let us hold space for our pain and our joy alike, embracing the full spectrum of human experience with compassion and grace.

For in the act of healing, we reclaim our power. We transform our pain into purpose, our wounds into wisdom. We emerge from the depths of our suffering, reborn and renewed, ready to embrace the fullness of life with open arms and open hearts. And though the journey may be long and arduous, with each step we take towards healing, we inch closer to the wholeness that resides within us all.

11. Breaking Free from the Loop: Rediscovering Purpose and Direction

As the writer of this exploration into the labyrinth of uncertainty and indecision, I extend a hand to guide you through the maze of life's perpetual loop cycles. We've all experienced those moments when we feel trapped, caught in a relentless cycle of indecision, unsure of which path to take or what action to pursue. It's as if we're spinning in circles, unable to break free from the grip of inertia and apathy. But fear not, for within the depths of our own consciousness lies the key to liberation and renewal.

Picture yourself standing at a crossroads, surrounded by countless pathways stretching out before you. Each route holds the promise of adventure, growth, and possibility, yet the sheer abundance of choices leaves you paralyzed with indecision. You find yourself stuck in a loop, endlessly cycling through the same patterns of thought and behavior, unable to move forward or backward. But here's the truth: the only way out of the loop is through self-awareness and intentional action. It requires a willingness to confront the underlying fears, doubts, and insecurities that keep us tethered to the familiar comforts of the status quo. It demands a courageous leap into the unknown, a willingness to embrace discomfort and uncertainty in pursuit of personal growth and transformation.

As the writer of your own narrative, you possess the power to rewrite the script and chart a new course for your life. Start by acknowledging the patterns that keep you trapped in the loop – the self-limiting beliefs, the fear of failure, the inertia of complacency. Shine a light on these shadows of the mind and reclaim control of your thoughts and actions.

Next, cultivate a sense of curiosity and openness to new experiences. Embrace the unknown with a spirit of adventure, knowing that growth and discovery await on the other side of fear. Take small steps outside your comfort zone, experiment with new ideas and pursuits, and trust in the wisdom of your intuition to guide you along the way.

Finally, surround yourself with a supportive community of like-minded individuals who uplift and inspire you to be the best version of yourself. Seek out mentors, friends, and allies who share your values and vision for the future and draw strength from their collective wisdom and encouragement.

In conclusion, dear reader, know that you are not alone in your journey through the loop. As the writer of your own narrative, you possess the power to break free from the shackles of indecision and rediscover your sense of purpose and direction. Embrace the unknown with courage and curiosity, trust in the wisdom of your intuition, and take intentional action to create the life you truly desire. For within the depths of uncertainty lies the promise of growth, transformation, and infinite possibility.

12. Cultivating Growth: Nurturing the Seeds of Potential

In the vast expanse of existence, growth is the ever-present force that propels us forward, urging us to reach towards the sunlit skies of our highest aspirations. It is a journey of evolution, a testament to the boundless potential that resides within each of us, waiting to be unearthed and cultivated. Like gardeners tending to the soil, we are tasked with nurturing the seeds of our own potential, providing them with the nourishment and care they need to thrive. This journey of growth begins with self-awareness—a willingness to look inward and confront the barriers that stand between us and our fullest expression of self. As we till the soil of our own consciousness, we uncover the roots of our limiting beliefs and self-imposed constraints, clearing the way for new growth to take root. It is a process of excavation, as we unearth the buried treasures of our own resilience and creativity, allowing them to blossom forth in the fertile ground of possibility. But growth is not a solitary endeavor; it is a communal act of co-creation, shaped by the influences of the world around us. We are nourished by the wisdom of those who have walked this path before us, drawing inspiration from their stories of triumph and transformation. And in turn, we become stewards of growth for others, lending our support and encouragement as they embark upon their own journeys of self-discovery. Yet, growth is not always easy. It requires patience and perseverance, a willingness to embrace the discomfort of stretching beyond our comfort zones. It demands resilience—the ability to weather the storms of adversity and emerge stronger on the other side. And above all, it requires courage—the courage to leap into the unknown, to trust in the process of becoming, even when the path ahead is shrouded in uncertainty.

But with each step we take towards growth, we inch closer to the fullest expression of ourselves, to the radiant bloom of our own potential. And though the journey may be fraught with challenges and setbacks, with each obstacle we overcome, we emerge more resilient, more empowered, and more deeply rooted in the truth of who we are. So let us embrace the journey of growth with open hearts and open minds, knowing that within each of us lies the seeds of greatness waiting to be cultivated. Let us tend to the garden of our own souls with care and intention, trusting in the transformative power of growth to lead us towards the fullest expression of our humanity. And in doing so, let us honor the sacred journey of becoming, knowing that with each passing day, we are one step closer to the radiant bloom of our own potential.

Moonlight Musings

Like the phases of the moon, our lives are marked by cycles of growth and change. Embrace each phase with courage, knowing that transformation awaits.

13. Lunar Luminescence: Finding Inspiration in the Moon's Mystique

The Moon, that familiar celestial companion, holds within its silent beauty an endless array of inspiration for humanity. From its serene glow illuminating the night sky to its enigmatic presence in the vastness of space, the Moon captivates our imagination and beckons us to explore realms beyond our earthly bounds.

One of the most profound ways the Moon inspires us is through its unwavering perseverance. For billions of years, it has faithfully orbited our planet, a silent witness to the ebb and flow of civilizations, the rise and fall of empires, and the evolution of life itself. In its consistency lies a lesson for us all: the power of resilience and determination in the face of adversity. Just as the Moon continues its eternal journey despite the challenges it encounters, so too can we find the strength to endure and overcome obstacles in our own lives.

Moreover, the Moon serves as a reminder of the boundless possibilities that lie beyond our current horizons. Its barren surface, marked by craters and ancient lava flows, serves as a testament to the potential for exploration and discovery in the uncharted realms of space. By gazing up at the Moon, we are reminded of humanity's innate curiosity and our insatiable desire to push the boundaries of knowledge and understanding. Furthermore, the Moon's influence extends beyond the realm of science and exploration, permeating the realms of art, literature, and culture. It has been a muse for poets and artists throughout history, inspiring countless works of creativity and imagination. Its ethereal beauty has sparked the imaginations of dreamers and visionaries, fueling a sense of wonder and awe that transcends time and space. In addition, the Moon serves as a symbol of unity and interconnectedness. No matter where we are in the world, we all share the same Moon in the sky above us. Its gentle light unites us in a shared experience, reminding us of our common humanity and the bonds that connect us across borders and cultures. In essence, the Moon serves as a beacon of inspiration, guiding us on a journey of exploration, discovery, and self-discovery. Its timeless beauty, unwavering perseverance, and universal appeal remind us of the limitless potential that lies within each of us, urging us to reach for the stars and embrace the wonders of the unknown. As we gaze up at the Moon, let us be inspired to dream, to explore, and to embark on our own journey of discovery, knowing that the possibilities are as vast and infinite as the cosmos itself.

14. Beyond Perfection

In a world where perfection is often held as the ultimate standard of success and happiness, it's easy to feel overwhelmed by the pressure to meet unrealistic expectations. We are bombarded daily with images of flawless beauty, unattainable achievements, and seemingly perfect lives plastered across social media feeds and glossy magazines. But what if I told you that beyond the facade of perfection lies a realm of true fulfillment and joy?

Life is messy, unpredictable, and wonderfully imperfect. It's in the moments of vulnerability, the cracks in the facade, that we find the beauty of authenticity. Think about it – when was the last time you felt truly alive, truly connected to the world around you? Was it in the meticulously curated highlight reel of someone else's life, or was it in the messy, chaotic, beautifully imperfect moments of your own?

As the writer of this journey, I've come to realize that true happiness lies not in the pursuit of perfection, but in the embrace of life's imperfections. It's in the laughter shared with friends over a spilled cup of coffee, the tears shed in moments of vulnerability, the love that blossoms in the wake of heartache. It's in the messy kitchen counters, the mismatched socks, the untamed curls – these are the things that make us uniquely human, beautifully flawed, and infinitely lovable.

So, let's shift our focus away from the unattainable ideal of perfection and instead celebrate the imperfect beauty of the present moment. Let's cultivate gratitude for the small joys that pepper our daily lives – a warm hug from a loved one, a breathtaking sunset, a kind word from a stranger. Let's embrace our quirks, our idiosyncrasies, our imperfections, knowing that they are what make us who we are.

As the author of your own story, I encourage you to rewrite the narrative of perfection that society has ingrained in us. Let go of the need to measure up to impossible standards and instead embrace the messy, unpredictable, wonderfully imperfect journey that is life. For it's in the acceptance of our flaws that we find true freedom, true happiness, and true connection with ourselves and the world around us.

Forward Bound: Teens Shaping Tomorrow

Each step taken today by teens echoes into the future they'll inherit. With purposeful strides and unwavering determination, they shape a path towards a brighter tomorrow.

15. The root cause of all the suffering

We live in a world of thought, not reality. "Thought is not reality; yet it is through thought that our realities are created. Each of us lives through our own perceptions of the world, which are vastly different from the person right next to us. An example of this is that you could be sitting in a coffee shop having a quarter-life existential crisis, completely stressed out of your mind about how you have no idea what you're doing with your life when it seems like everyone else has theirs together, while the person next to you is happily enjoying their freshly brewed drink while peacefully people watching. You both are in the same exact coffee shop, smelling the same aroma, surrounded by the same strangers, but how the world looks to both of you couldn't be more different. Many of us go through the exact same events or are in the same location at the same time yet are having completely different experiences of the world.

Here's another example of how we live in a world of thought and not reality. If you walk up to 100 different people and ask each of them what money means to them, how many different answers do you think you'll get? Close to 100 different answers! Money is technically the same thing, but it means something different to each person. Money could mean time, freedom, opportunity, security, peace of mind, or it could mean evil, greed, and the reason why people commit crimes. For now, I'm not going to get into which one is right or wrong (hint: there is no right or wrong answer, but that's for a different chapter). Another illustration of this concept is as follows: If you survey 100 different people and ask each of them what they think of our current president, how many different answers do you think you'll get? Even though it is the same exact person we're talking about, we will get 100 different answers because most people live in their own thoughts and perceptions of the world. The meaning (or thinking) we give an event is what determines how we ultimately feel about it. That meaning or thinking is the filter through which we see life from then on — because of this, we live through a perception of reality, not in reality itself. Reality is that the event happened, with no meaning, thinking, or interpretation of it. Any meaning or thinking we give the event is on us and that is how our perception of reality is created. This is how our experience of life is created from the inside out. It's not about the events that happen in our lives, but our interpretation of them, which causes us to feel good or bad about something. This is how people in third world countries can be happier than people in first world countries and people in first world countries can be more miserable than people in third world countries. Our feelings do not come from external events, but from our own thinking about the events. Therefore, we can only ever feel what we are thinking. Let's hypothetically say that you really hate your job, and it causes you an enormous amount of stress, anxiety, and frustration. It pains you to even set foot in the building where you work and just thinking about your job makes you furious. When you're thinking about your job, you're just sitting there on a sofa with your family watching a TV show together, but you are fuming at the thought of your job. Everyone else is having a good time, except you. In this moment, everyone else in your family is having a different experience of life than you, even though the same event is happening. Just the thought of work created a whole different perception of reality, even though you're not physically at work. If it were true that external events cause us to feel the way we feel inside, then you should be a happy camper in your living room, watching a funny TV show with your family every single time you do this activity — but that's not the case. Now, you may be saying that you're only feeling this way because an external event, your job, is causing you to feel stressed and anxious. To that I'll ask the question, is it absolutely true that every single person feels the exact same way about the job they're working in?

Two different people can be doing the exact same job but will have completely different experiences of that job. It can be the most amazing experience and a dream job for one person but be another person's worst nightmare and living hell. The only difference between one person and the other is how they think about their job, which determines how they ultimately feel about it. Now let's go back to the original scenario of you hypothetically hating your job. Remember how much stress, anxiety, and frustration it causes you when you think about it? Let's do a quick thought experiment about that by answering the question below: Who would you be without that thought that you hated your job? Take 1 minute to see what comes up for you and don't move on until you do that. If you don't overthink it and truly let the answers surface from within you, without that thought, you will most likely feel and be happy, peaceful, free, and light. Without our usual thinking about a particular event or thing, our experience of it completely alters. This is how we live in a world of thought, not reality, and how our perception of reality is created from the inside out, through our own thinking. With this new understanding, you've just uncovered the cause of all our human psychological suffering...

The root cause of our suffering is our own thinking. Now before you throw this book across the room and light it on fire, I'm not saying that this is all in our heads and that it isn't real. Our perception of reality is very real. We will feel what we think, and our feelings are real. That is completely undeniable. However, our thinking will look like an inevitable, unchangeable reality to us until we begin seeing how our reality is created. If we know that we can only ever feel what we are thinking, then we know that we can change our feelings by changing our thinking. Thus, we can change our experience of life by knowing that it comes from our own thinking. And if that is true, then we are ever only one thought away from experiencing something different and transforming our entire lives at any moment — through a state of no thought. In short, the moment we stop thinking is when our happiness begins.

16. Why do we even think?

"I think and think and think, I've thought myself out of happiness one million times, but never once into it."

We as humans have evolved to develop a sophisticated ability to rationalize, analyze, and think because it simply helped us survive. Our minds do an incredible job to keep us alive, but it does not help us thrive. It is concerned solely with our safety and survival, but not our fulfillment or joy. The mind's job is to alert us of potential dangers in our environment that may threaten our lives. It does its job so well that not only will it scan our immediate surroundings for threats, but it will even reference our backlog of past experiences to create hypothetical scenarios and predict what it thinks could be future potential dangers based on our memories. None of this is wrong by any means. The mind is simply doing what it was designed to do. When we don't understand that its only duty is to help us survive, then we will get angry and frustrated with it. All conflict is derived from an innocent misunderstanding. Our mind's duty is to keep us alive. Our consciousness's duty is to help us feel fulfilled. Your soul is the reason why you're even on this journey in the first place — to find peace, love, and joy for yourself. Your mind has done an amazing job at what it was made to do, but now you may relieve it of its job because we no longer live in the wild where death could be right around the corner in a bush. If we keep using our minds, we will constantly stay in a state of fight or flight, anxiety, fear, frustration, depression, anger, resentment, and all negative emotions because the mind thinks everything is a threat to our very existence. If you want to be free, happy, peaceful, and full of love, then you will need to let go of listening only to your mind and go beyond it by tuning into something much greater that will help you not just to survive, but to thrive. "

17. If we stop thinking, What do we do about our goals, dreams and ambitions?

""There are no limitations to the mind except those we acknowledge.""

I think, therefore I suffer

When I finally understood that thinking was the root cause of all of my suffering, I was jumping up and down, exhilarated, relieved and grateful for discovering the true reason for everything negative I've experienced in my life. This ecstasy was short-lived though because soon after the exuberance settled, the next thoughts popped into my mind: If thinking is the root cause of all my suffering and I just stop thinking, how do I live my life now? What about all of my goals, dreams, and ambitions? Do I stop wanting things in life? Will I just devolve into a couch potato and not do anything with my life anymore? In case you were wondering, yes, I am telepathic and yes, I can read your mind. Just kidding, but if you are wondering how I wrote the exact or very similar questions and know what thoughts you most likely have right now, it's because I am human also, contrary to popular belief. All of us are going through similar journeys of awakening to our True Selves, so rest assured that many people are having the exact same thoughts you are having right now as you come to see your true magnificence. Now back to the question of what we do about our goals, dreams, and ambitions if we stop thinking. As I pondered on these questions, an incredible amount of fear and anxiety began to surface because I thought that I would have to give all of it up and become a monk in the middle of the mountains. I was definitely not ready to do that. As much as I wish I were that enlightened and detached from my life, I genuinely enjoyed being in the world, experiencing the fullness of life with other people, even if a large portion of my life was filled with suffering. Here's what I've discovered about what to do with our goals and dreams with this new understanding. As we've mentioned in previous chapters, there's a difference between thoughts versus thinking. The source of thoughts and the source of thinking are different, and the source is what will dictate whether it causes suffering or not. Similarly, where our goals and dreams come from will determine whether we feel great about pursuing them or not. Like everything in this world, there is nothing inherently good or bad, only our thinking makes it so. Goals, dreams, and ambitions are not good or bad, so it's not really an either-or situation, but more about where those goals are coming from.

<u>There are two sources of goals: goals created out of inspiration and goals created out of desperation.</u>

When goals are created out of desperation, we feel a large sense of scarcity and urgency. It feels heavy, like a burden, we may even feel daunted by the colossal task we've just committed ourselves to, imposter syndrome and self-doubt begin to manifest, and we always feel like we never have enough time for anything. We go about our life frantically, desperately searching for answers and ways that we can accomplish our goal faster, always looking externally, never feeling enough or that we can ever get enough. Worst of all, if we happen to accomplish our goal, within a few hours or days afterwards, all of those same feelings of lack begin to resurface. We begin not feeling content with what we have done, unable to savor our accomplishments and because what we did never feels like it's enough, we feel that same way about ourselves. Not knowing what else to do, we look around for guidance externally to see what others are doing and see they're continuing to do the same thing. Thus, we go ahead and proceed to set another goal out of desperation in an attempt to escape all of the negative feelings gnawing away at our soul. When we dig a little deeper into these types of goals we set, they are all typically "means goals" and not "end goals". In other words, the goals we set in this state of desperation are all a means to an end. There's always a reason we want to accomplish the goal and it's always for something else. For example, we want to create a multi-million-dollar business because we want financial freedom, or we want to quit our job so that we can escape the stress and anxiety that comes from it. We feel like we HAVE to do these things instead of WANT to. Goals created from desperation are typically "realistic" and created from analyzing our past and what we think to be "plausible" in the moment. It feels very confining and limiting. Although these types of goals and dreams may excite us in the moment, as soon as we begin to try to create it, we feel a lack, and we are desperate to bring the dream to life. Paradoxically, if we do end up achieving a goal created out of desperation, we end up feeling even more empty than we did before it. The next "logical" thing we tend to do is to set an even bigger goal out of even greater desperation to hopefully make us feel whole inside. This is how most of us set our goals and how we live our lives. I'm also not saying this to criticize or judge at all, but to reveal the reality of it. The only reason why I was able to describe it in painful and excruciating detail was because that was my life. Here's the good news: it's not your fault that you set goals that way if you are and there's a way out. It's through creating goals and dreams out of inspiration instead of desperation. When we create goals out of inspiration versus desperation, it is a completely different story. In this state, we are creating because we feel deeply moved, inspired, and expansive. It feels like a calling rather than an obligation. It is like there's a powerful force of life coming from within us, wanting to be expressed through us to be made manifested into the physical world. This is why painters paint, why dancers dance, why writers write and why singers sing, even if they never get paid or make a living from it. We feel pulled by a force to create something. We gravitate towards it. We feel compelled to do it. When we feel like this, we are creating from a place of abundance instead of lack. Most surprising of all is that in this state, we are creating not for any reason at all, other than because we simply want to. We don't create because we feel like we HAVE to. We create because we simply want to and there's no other reason. We aren't creating these goals so that we can do something else or use it as a means to get something else we want. This creating comes from a place of wholeness and abundance. It's an overflowing of love and joy for life. This is the reason why most of us want or have kids. It's not so that we can milk our kids for their money once they're old enough to work and hopefully use them as a retirement plan. We want to have kids because we want to share the abundance of what we have with them, and it comes from a place of sharing what we have lots of versus trying to get something out of them. This feeling of deep inspiration is incredibly difficult to describe because it does not come from this world. It really doesn't come from us, but through us from something greater than us. I like to call this feeling divine inspiration because the ideas and vision we have of what we want to create seem to be far bigger than we could have possibly imagined or come up with ourselves. Since divine inspiration doesn't come from us but from something greater, it doesn't analyze or rely on past data or what you or anyone in the world has already accomplished. Divine inspiration is what happens when groundbreaking creations and inventions are created that seemed to be impossible not too long ago. It knows no boundaries, limits, or constraints. It is an incredibly expansive force that energizes and lifts us, making us feel like we're "high" on life. In this state, we feel whole, complete, filled with unconditional love, joy, and peace. We don't analyze, compare, criticize, judge, or rationalize anything, but instead we truly live, love, share, give, create, grow, and nourish. It really is one of the greatest feelings we can experience, and it is truly a gift that we can experience the divine as humans (and it's because we're from the same source). Everyone has experienced this deep feeling and desire to create something marvelous in the world that's out of pure inspiration and not desperation. Before moving on to the next paragraph, I encourage you to test this theory. Pause here and spend a few minutes thinking about times in your life where you felt an overwhelming feeling and desire to create something magnificent because you felt deeply inspired and called to. It doesn't matter if you actually created it or not, but just think of a time where you felt that feeling to create out of inspiration. Isn't that just one of the most amazing feelings in the entire world? Most of us feel this divine inspiration, but then suppress it as soon as we begin thinking about doing it. We begin to think ourselves into doubt, rationalize why we can't do it, tell ourselves that it is unrealistic, how we should focus on more important things, and that we're not good enough to do it. As soon as we begin to think about the thought of us wanting to create, it completely shuts off the source of that inspiration and we go back to living life as usual. When we cut off that source, we also cut off the feelings of abundance, exuberance, ecstasy, joy, pure unconditional love, and go back to the feelings of doubt, anxiety, frustration, sadness, and feel confined, stuck, and frustrated with our lives. We can only ever follow one calling at a time, either inspiration or desperation in the present moment. The two cannot coexist at the same time, but we can fluctuate between the two depending on how much thinking is going on. When we stop thinking, we don't stop having goals and dreams, we actually fall back into our true nature and begin to create goals and dreams out of inspiration versus desperation. We begin to allow thoughts from the Universe to come into our mind that lead us to divine inspiration to create something that has never been created before in the world. When we follow divine inspiration, we feel alive, whole, joy, love, peace, and fulfillment.

So how can we tell when a goal or dream is created out of inspiration or desperation?

A simple way to know if a goal or dream is created out of inspiration is to remember the distinction between thoughts and thinking. Goals and dreams that come in the form of thought are created out of inspiration. Goals and dreams that come from thinking are created out of desperation. Typically, when we think, we'll analyze, judge, criticize, rationalize, and use our past to try to create our new goals, but this form of creating goals feels extremely restricting and limiting. We don't typically feel good when creating these types of goals and when we're pursuing them, we do not feel great either, since it's all out of desperation. Another way to identify the two is to sense how you feel energetically. Goals and dreams created out of desperation will feel very heavy, draining, confining, and empty. We tend to feel a lot of scarcity, fear, and stress, like we HAVE to do it or that we are obligated to. With these types of goals, it seems like if we do not accomplish it, that there will be dire consequences, hence the high pressure and stakes (I'm sure you can see now how this can create the feeling of desperation). Moreover, we feel like we're trying to accomplish these goals to escape our current situation and get out of something. Our goals created in this state are typically means goals, meaning that we want to achieve these goals so that we can do something else afterwards, such as having the goal to quit our job. Most likely you'll have this goal because you want to go do something you actually enjoy, but you can see how the goal of quitting your job is just a means goal for you to go do something else. Or having a goal of making $1 million is typically set because you want to have financial freedom and go travel the world. These goals are always a means to an end and not the end itself. There's always a reason that we want to accomplish these goals and it makes us feel very empty inside. I want to emphasize that none of these goals are inherently bad or that we shouldn't have goals of wanting to make money or quitting our jobs. If those goals are created from inspiration, that is completely different. It just depends on the source of the goals and not necessarily the goal itself. This is an important distinction to make, otherwise you'll spend most of your time debating and stressing yourself out over if this is the right goal for you or not. There is no right or wrong goal, only goals created from inspiration or desperation. It just depends on how you want to feel inside and when you're aware of these two types of goals and how they manifest, then you'll be able to feel blissful as you go about creating amazing things in your life.

On the other hand, goals and dreams created out of inspiration (which comes from thought) feel very light, energizing, uplifting, and expansive. We tend to feel excited, joyful, and most importantly, inspired. We don't feel like we HAVE to create it, but that we WANT to. Instead of feeling like you NEED to do this, you feel inspired to. There is virtually no pressure because we're not trying to get out of something or escape our current situation by accomplishing this goal. There is no scarcity or urgency because we don't feel like we're creating from a place of lack, but instead from a place of abundance and we just want to share it with the world. Since it's coming from inspiration, we are not doing it to get something out of it so that we can do something else. It's not a means goal, but simply an end in and of itself. There is no "reason" we need to create it. We are not creating so that we can feel whole, but we are creating because we feel whole and want to give from that place, not expecting anything from it. I'm sure you can see the stark difference between the two now and that you can tell which type your goals currently fall under. If most of your goals fall under the category of desperation, don't worry because most people have goals created from desperation, including myself before I knew a better way. So how do we create goals and dreams out of inspiration versus desperation? Creating goals and dreams from divine inspiration isn't something you have to try to do. We naturally have thoughts of infinite inspiration all the time. If you look at children, they naturally have the wildest dreams and imaginations of what they want to do. It almost doesn't even register in their minds that they can't do something most of the time. The only difference between us and children is that we have learned to shut down all these thoughts of inspiration which contain our dreams, hopes, and goals that we truly want to see manifested in the world. Our minds are filled more with reasons of why we can't than thoughts of what we want to create. We innately have an infinite flow of inspiration that comes through us, but we block that flow as soon as we begin thinking about the thoughts we have, which causes self-doubt, self-sabotage, and anxiety. Think of the flow of inspiration to create like a river. The river always flows until man puts something there to block it, like a dam. Then when the dam is there, we ask why there are so many fish dying, animals disappearing, and forests dwindling, when all we need to do was return the river back to its natural state and everything will be working perfectly fine, the way nature intended it to. This is the same for our minds and our goals. We always dream, have big goals, and know what to do at all times when we're tapped into our inner wisdom and inner intelligence, free from thinking. If we simply do not think about our thoughts, any sort of thoughts about dreams, goals, and desires that naturally arise are all from the divine and that is how you "create" goals out of inspiration versus desperation.

A question that greatly helps me to settle the thinking and tap into the limitless well of possibilities of what I could create is: "If I had infinite money, already traveled the world, had no fear, and didn't receive any recognition for what I do, what would I do or what would I create?" Whenever we ask questions, answers always arise. It is impossible for our brains to hear a question and not come up with a response. So when you ask yourself this question, whatever begins to come up for you without any manual thinking will be from the divine and from inspiration versus desperation. The way the question is worded is extremely important because it removes most of the thinking, fear, criticism, and external reasons of why you would want to do something, so it focuses your answer on what you truly want to create (usually it's for no reason other than you just wanting to create it because it's fun), without any influences from the material world. Try asking the question and seeing what comes up for you! You'll be surprised at what surfaces, but don't get caught up with your thinking when those true dreams of yours begin to be revealed to you.

   - To a mind without the limits of thinking, anything is possible.

Solitude's Brilliance

Amidst the quiet of solitude, one discovers not loneliness, but the uncharted territory of self-discovery, where every solitary step illuminates the path to one's own radiant brilliance.

18. Nothing is either good or bad

Here's an analogy that helps put this into perspective. On a piano, there are 88 keys. When we look at a piano, we don't point out specific keys for no reason and say that that key is "wrong". We only think a specific key is "wrong", if we think someone is playing a specific song and hits a key that isn't in the song. Inherently, the piano has no wrong keys though. There are only keys and notes that sound more or less pleasant when played consecutively. Just like how there are no wrong keys on the piano, there are no "wrong" decisions in life. There's only thinking that give us pleasant or not so pleasant feelings. When we put things into a bucket of right or wrong, good or bad, this creates duality and conditions in our lives, which determines how we feel. For instance, if we believe that that opposing political parties are wrong or bad, this can cause animosity within us and make us feel a concoction of negative emotions. If, on the other hand, we see different political parties in the same way as there are different keys on the piano and how there are no inherently "wrong" parties, then we open ourselves up to experience love, joy, and peace in the moment. We begin to see alternative perspectives that we haven't seen before and have an opportunity to deepen our understanding of the true nature of life. It's like if we are hiking on a mountain and stop at specific points to look at the beautiful view. There are no "wrong" spots that we can stop at, stand in, and take in the magnificence of nature, but by being open to all possible spots we can stand in, we can see the view from different vantage points we haven't seen from before. Instead of looking for right or wrong, good or bad in the world, look for truth. Instead of trying to prove we are right and they are wrong, or how they're better and we're worse, look for the truth in what's in front of you. I would only caution this by saying that many people believe what they think is the truth. For the most part, without this deeper understanding of life, most of what we think is not truth, even though it may seem like it. True truth is not subjective. If it is "true" for one person, but not for another, then it is not universal truth. Look for what is universally true for every single conscious human being on the planet, no matter who they are, where they're from, and what their background is. That is the true truth and that is where you'll find everything you've been searching for. Remember that the only place you can find this is deep within your being, so don't try to go looking for it outside of you. If you're confronted with something that may stir up negative emotions, go within yourself to find the source of universal truth deep within your soul. If you try to look for the answers outside or try to dig into external reasons for the root of why you feel this way, you will be looking for the rest of eternity and will never find it. Negative emotions are an indication of misunderstanding.

When we are gripped by negative emotions, it means that we believe what we are thinking. It is in this moment that we simply forgot where our experience comes from and that our thinking is the cause of our negative emotions. All you have to do is remember that thinking is the root cause of how we're feeling. Once this is brought into your awareness, don't fight the thinking. Just become aware that it is your thinking that's causing the ill feelings, welcome it with love, and it will slowly dissipate before your eyes. Not too long after, you'll return to your natural state of peace, love, and joy.

-"There is nothing either good or bad but thinking makes it so."

19. Now What?

Although this is the end of the book, it is just the beginning of a new life for you. You are only ever one thought away from peace, love, and joy — which come from a state of non-thinking. Remember this and keep it close to your heart because it is all the hope you need when life gets inevitably tough. In the beginning, I promised you that you will not be the same person as you were before you read this book. If you began reading this book with the intention of having an open and willing mind, then you have already received numerous insights that have completely changed the way you look at life and thus you are not the same person as you were before. Once you see something new from an insight, you cannot unsee it. Once your consciousness expands, it cannot contract again. We may forget from time to time and cause ourselves to suffer when we begin thinking again, but as soon as we remember that, we immediately realize that we are the ever-expanding awareness of life itself and find love, peace, and joy in the present. If this seems like it is too simple and that it can't be all there is, that is just your mind causing you to think again. The truth is simple and will always be. Anything that makes something complex and intricate is only taking you further away from the truth. The truth is not something you think, but something that you know and feel deep in your soul. Listen to that still inner wisdom inside of you that knows all of this. Let it guide you through your life. We are most fulfilled when we listen to our soul. The world will continuously advertise to us that we are not enough, that we are missing something or don't have everything we want. People will constantly bombard you with their own opinions, judgements, and advice. Know that they are innocently caught up in their thinking and thank them for caring, but do not fall into the illusion that you need any of that. Everything you could possibly ever want and need is already inside of you. You are already all of the love, joy, peace, and fulfillment you have ever wanted. It is only when we forget that fact and get caught up in our thinking that we do not see it. Continue to live in this state of pure peace and let go of any thinking that may pop up in your mind. The longer you stay in this space, the more miracles will show up in your life. Although you can go and share this message with every person you meet, you won't even need to because they will notice something completely different about you. You'll be glowing, vibrant, and emanating pure love and joy — and they will begin asking why and how. You are now equipped with everything you need to know on how to stop your own psychological suffering and embody a state of peace, love, and joy, which is always available to you at all times. There's a good chance that you have already experienced the bliss of knowing and being this.

20. Healing Through Acceptance: Breaking Free from Self-Harm for Others

In the dimly lit corners of our minds, we often find ourselves tangled in a web of self-sacrifice, believing that our worth lies in how much we can endure for the sake of others. We hurt ourselves, both physically and emotionally, believing that it somehow serves a greater purpose – to alleviate the pain of those we love, to keep peace at any cost, to fulfill expectations placed upon us by society or by ourselves. Yet, in this cycle of self-harm, we often forget the most important person in the equation: ourselves.

It's a paradoxical truth that in our quest to protect and care for others, we end up neglecting our own well-being. We convince ourselves that our pain is insignificant compared to the burdens carried by those around us. We minimize our struggles, burying them deep beneath the surface, lest they disrupt the delicate balance of the lives we hold dear. But in doing so, we only perpetuate a cycle of suffering, both for ourselves and for those we seek to protect. The journey to healing begins with a simple yet profound act:

acceptance. Acceptance of ourselves, exactly as we are, flaws and all. Acceptance of our emotions, our vulnerabilities, our limitations. Acceptance of the fact that we are human, imperfect beings deserving of love and compassion, both from others and from ourselves. When we embrace acceptance, we release ourselves from the shackles of self-blame and self-judgment. We recognize that it's okay to not be okay, that our worth is not contingent upon our ability to meet impossible standards of perfection. We acknowledge that our pain is valid, deserving of acknowledgment and care, rather than dismissal or suppression. Acceptance doesn't mean resignation or complacency. It's not about giving up or giving in. Rather, it's about-facing reality head-on, with courage and compassion. It's about acknowledging the truth of our experiences, without judgment or resistance. It's about making peace with the past, embracing the present, and trusting in the possibilities of the future. In accepting ourselves, we pave the way for healing to begin. We open ourselves up to the possibility of growth, of transformation, of becoming the best versions of ourselves. We reclaim our power, recognizing that we have the agency to shape our own lives, to set boundaries, to prioritize our own well-being.

So, let us take a moment to pause, to breathe, to offer ourselves the gift of acceptance. Let us release the burden of self-blame, of self-sacrifice, of self-harm. Let us embrace ourselves with love and kindness, knowing that we are worthy of healing, of happiness, of a life lived authentically and unapologetically. And as we embark on this journey of self-discovery and self-compassion, may we shine our light brightly, illuminating the path for others to follow.

21. Starting Anew Through Acceptance

Saying goodbye is never easy. Whether it's parting ways with a friend, a loved one, or even a familiar phase of our lives, the act of leaving can be accompanied by a whirlwind of emotions – sadness, nostalgia, uncertainty. Yet, amidst the bittersweet symphony of farewells, lies the promise of new beginnings, of fresh opportunities waiting to be embraced. Leaving others behind often feels like navigating uncharted waters, fraught with doubt and apprehension. We may find ourselves grappling with feelings of guilt, wondering if our departure will leave a void in the lives of those we leave behind. We may fear the unknown, uncertain of what lies ahead and whether we have the strength to face it alone. However, it's in these moments of transition that we can embark on a journey of self-discovery and growth. The key to moving forward lies in acceptance – accepting that change is a natural part of life, that goodbyes are inevitable, and that holding onto the past only impedes our progress. Acceptance is not about denying our emotions or suppressing our grief; rather, it's about acknowledging the reality of the situation and choosing to embrace it with an open heart and mind. When we embrace acceptance, we free ourselves from the shackles of attachment and expectation. We release ourselves from the burden of trying to control outcomes beyond our grasp and instead focus on what we can control – our thoughts, our actions, our attitude towards change. We recognize that by letting go of what no longer serves us, we create space for new experiences, new connections, and new possibilities to enter our lives. Starting a new journey begins with a single step – a leap of faith into the unknown, guided by the belief that we are capable of navigating whatever challenges lie ahead. It's about trusting in our resilience, our adaptability, and our capacity for growth. It's about embracing uncertainty as an opportunity for adventure, rather than a source of fear. As we bid farewell to the familiar and set out on a new path, let us do so with grace and gratitude. Let us honor the memories and lessons learned from those we leave behind, while also embracing the excitement of what lies ahead. Let us trust that the universe has a plan for us, even if it's not immediately clear, and have faith that everything happens for a reason.

So, let us take a deep breath, gather our courage, and step boldly into the unknown. For it's in the act of leaving that we create space for new beginnings to unfold. And by embracing acceptance, we pave the way for a journey filled with possibility, growth, and endless opportunity.

22. Echoes of Betrayal

Friendship is often heralded as one of life's greatest treasures – a source of joy, companionship, and unwavering support. Yet, amidst the laughter and camaraderie, lies a truth that many of us are reluctant to acknowledge friendship can hurt. Despite our best intentions, our closest relationships have the potential to wound us in ways we never imagined. We invest our time, our energy, and our emotions into our friendships, trusting that they will endure the tests of time and circumstance. We confide in our friends, sharing our hopes, our dreams, and our deepest fears, believing that they will hold our secrets close and our hearts even closer. But sometimes, despite our best efforts, friendships falter, leaving us feeling betrayed, abandoned, and alone. Perhaps it's a friend who drifts away, gradually growing distant until they're little more than a distant memory. Or maybe it's a friend who betrays our trust, revealing our vulnerabilities to the world or turning their back on us when we need them most. Whatever the cause, the pain of a fractured friendship can cut deep, leaving scars that linger long after the wounds have healed. It's in these moments of heartache that we're faced with a difficult truth: relying too heavily on others for our happiness is a risky proposition. Placing our worth and our well-being in the hands of someone else leaves us vulnerable to disappointment and disillusionment when they inevitably fall short of our expectations. It's a painful lesson to learn, but an important one, nonetheless. Yet, in the midst of our pain, lies an opportunity for growth and self-discovery. For it's in the crucible of adversity that we come to understand our own strength and resilience. It's in the aftermath of a broken friendship that we learn to rely on ourselves for validation and support, rather than seeking it from external sources. Learning to stand on our own two feet doesn't mean shutting ourselves off from the world or becoming hardened and cynical. It simply means recognizing that while friendships can enrich our lives in countless ways, they are not the sole source of our happiness or fulfillment. True happiness comes from within, from cultivating a sense of self-worth and self-love that is independent of external validation.

So, the next time a friendship leaves you feeling bruised and battered, remember that it's not a reflection of your worth or your value as a person. It's simply a reminder that friendships, like all relationships, are complex and imperfect. And while they may hurt us in the end, they also have the power to teach us valuable lessons about ourselves and the world around us.

So, stop relying solely on others for your happiness and start cultivating a sense of self-reliance and resilience that will carry you through life's inevitable ups and downs. It's a long story, filled with twists and turns, but in the end, it's a journey worth taking.

The Mystique of Eyes

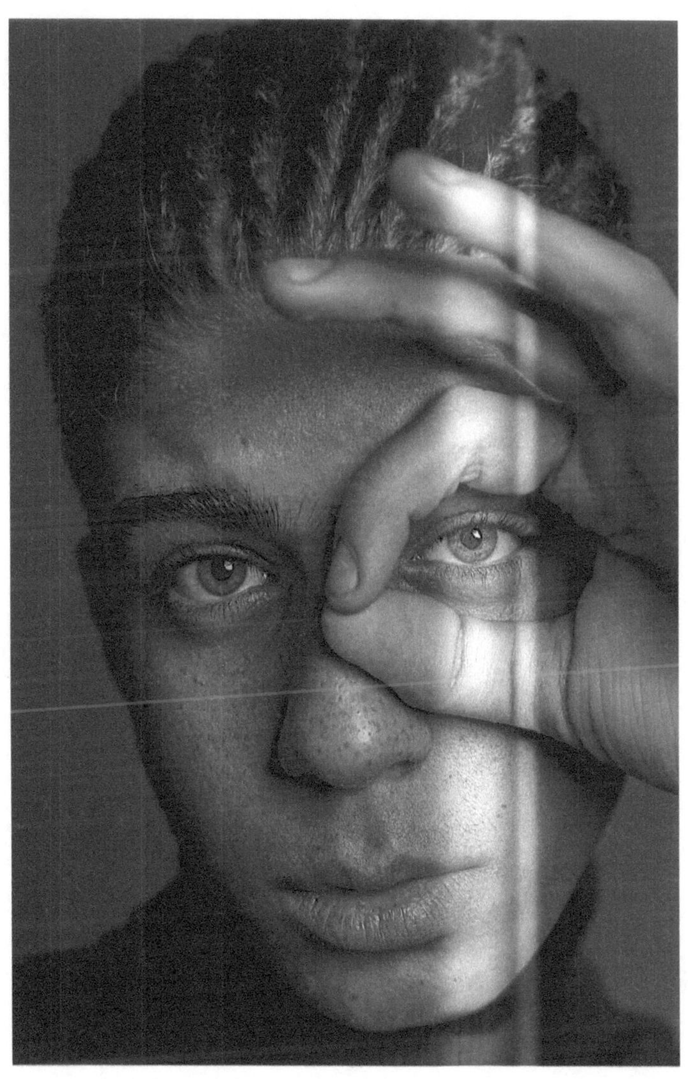

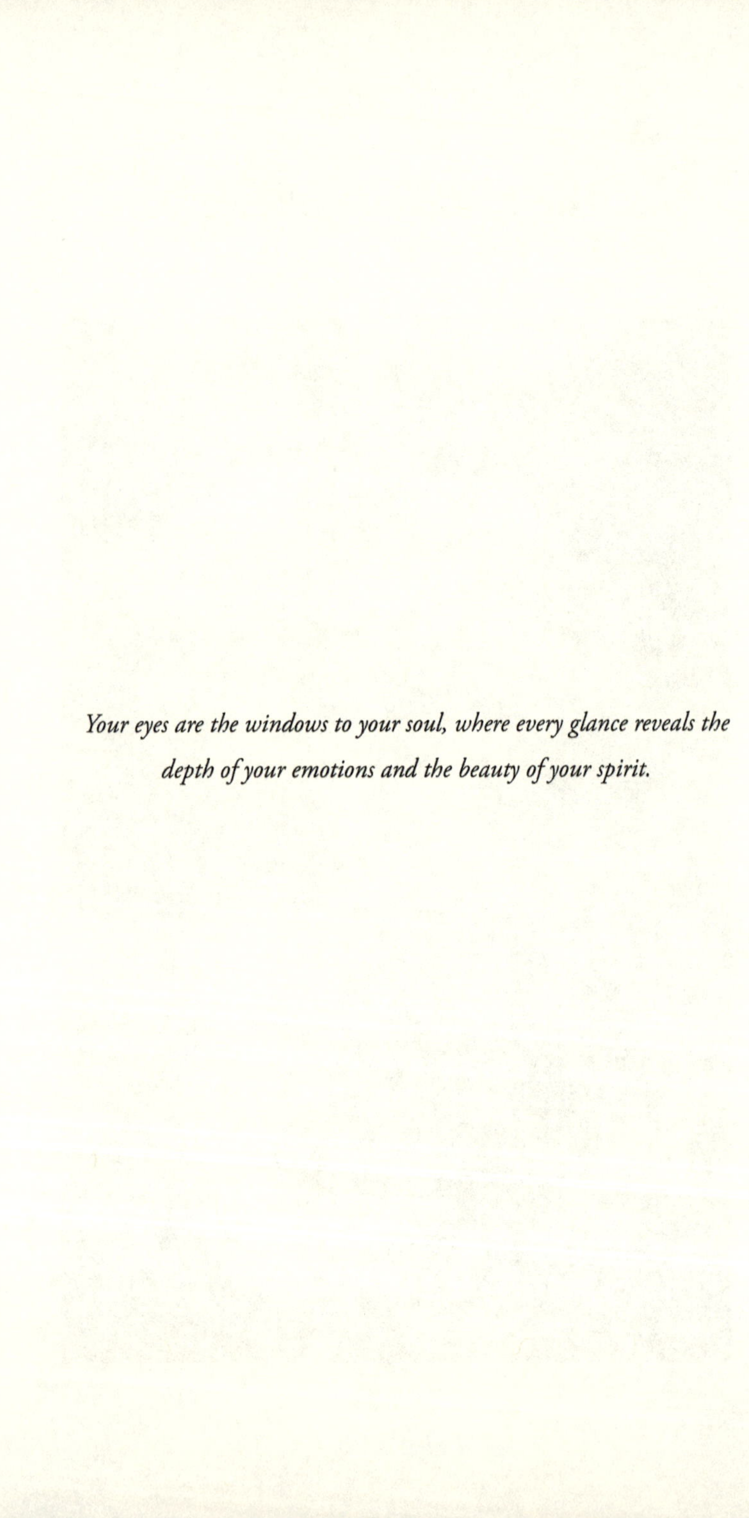

Your eyes are the windows to your soul, where every glance reveals the depth of your emotions and the beauty of your spirit.

23. Breaking Free from Negativity

Within each of us resides a spirit yearning to break free from the shackles of negativity that bind it. Like a caged bird longing for the open sky, our souls crave liberation from the heavy burdens of doubt, fear, and self-limiting beliefs that weigh us down. Yet, achieving this freedom requires courage, resilience, and a willingness to confront the darkness within.

The journey to freeing our spirits from negativity begins with self-awareness – a deep, honest examination of the thoughts, emotions, and patterns of behavior that hold us captive. It requires us to shine a light into the darkest corners of our minds, confronting our fears and insecurities with unwavering resolve. Only by acknowledging the existence of negativity can we hope to overcome its grip on our lives. Once we have identified the sources of negativity within ourselves, we can begin the process of transformation. This involves cultivating a mindset of positivity and resilience, replacing self-doubt with self-confidence, and fear with courage. It requires us to challenge negative thought patterns and replace them with empowering beliefs that affirm our worth and potential.

Practicing self-love and self-compassion is essential on this journey. It means treating us with kindness and understanding, especially in moments of struggle or setback.

By embracing our flaws and imperfections with acceptance and grace, we can weaken the hold that negativity has over us and create space for healing and growth. Surrounding ourselves with positivity is also crucial. This means seeking out uplifting environments, nurturing relationships, and sources of inspiration that uplift and energize us. It involves letting go of toxic influences and negative energy drains that sap our vitality and diminish our spirits. Forgiveness is a powerful tool for freeing ourselves from negativity. This includes forgiving others who have wronged us, but perhaps more importantly, forgiving ourselves for past mistakes and shortcomings. By releasing the weight of resentment and guilt, we create space for peace and healing to enter our lives. Finally, embracing a practice of gratitude and mindfulness can help to anchor us in the present moment, where negativity has less power to take hold. By cultivating an attitude of gratitude for the blessings in our lives, we shift our focus away from what is lacking and towards what is abundant and meaningful.

In the end, freeing our spirits from negativity is an ongoing journey, not a destination. It requires dedication, patience, and a commitment to personal growth. Yet, with each step we take towards liberation, we reclaim a little more of our true selves – resilient, courageous, and infinitely capable of overcoming any obstacle that stands in our way.

24. Unraveling the Mind: Breaking the Chains of Overthinking

In the labyrinth of the mind, overthinking casts its tangled web, ensnaring our thoughts in a relentless cycle of worry, doubt, and analysis paralysis. Like a persistent whisper in the ear, it feeds on uncertainty and fear, weaving a tapestry of imagined scenarios and catastrophic outcomes that threaten to overwhelm our sanity. Yet, within the depths of our consciousness lies the key to breaking free from its suffocating grip. The journey to unraveling the mind begins with awareness – a conscious recognition of the destructive patterns of overthinking that govern our thoughts and actions. It requires us to step back and observe our mental processes with detachment, acknowledging the relentless chatter of the inner critic and the grip of anxiety that tightens with each passing moment. Once we have identified the presence of overthinking in our lives, we can begin the process of disentanglement. This involves challenging the validity of our anxious thoughts and questioning the assumptions that underlie them. It requires us to differentiate between productive problem-solving and rumination, recognizing when our mental gymnastics serves no purpose other than to perpetuate our distress.

Practicing mindfulness is essential on this journey. It means learning to anchor us in the present moment, where overthinking has less power to take hold. By focusing our attention on the sensations of the breath or the sights and sounds of our surroundings, we can interrupt the cycle of rumination and bring ourselves back to a place of calm and clarity. Setting boundaries with our thoughts is also crucial. This involves recognizing when our minds are spiraling into overdrive and consciously choosing to redirect our attention elsewhere. It means giving ourselves permission to take breaks from the incessant chatter of the mind, whether through meditation, exercise, or engaging in activities that bring us joy and fulfillment.

Cultivating self-compassion is vital on this journey. It means treating us with kindness and understanding, especially in moments of overwhelm or self-criticism. By acknowledging our humanity and embracing our imperfections with warmth and acceptance, we can weaken the grip of overthinking and create space for peace and tranquility to enter our lives. Learning to let go of control is perhaps the most challenging aspect of breaking free from overthinking. It involves surrendering to the illusion of certainty and embracing the inherent unpredictability of life. It requires us to trust in our ability to navigate whatever challenges come our way, knowing that we are resilient and resourceful beings capable of weathering any storm.

In the end, unraveling the mind is a journey of self-discovery and self-empowerment. It requires courage, patience, and a willingness to confront the shadows that lurk within. Yet, with each step we take towards liberation, we reclaim a little more of our mental clarity and inner peace – untethered from the chains of overthinking and free to embrace the fullness of our existence.

25. Harnessing the Power of Failure

Failure, with its sting of disappointment and its shadow of doubt, often looms large in the landscape of our lives. It is a bitter pill to swallow, a reminder of our fallibility and our vulnerability to the whims of fate. Yet, within the depths of failure lies the potential for growth, resilience, and ultimately, success. It is in the face of failure that we are presented with a choice – to succumb to despair or to rise above adversity with grace and determination.

The journey to embracing setbacks begins with a shift in perspective – a reframing of failure as an opportunity for learning and growth rather than a mark of inadequacy or defeat. It requires us to challenge the notion that failure is something to be feared or avoided at all costs and instead, to embrace it as an inevitable part of the human experience. Once we have embraced the inevitability of failure, we can begin the process of reframing our perceptions of success and failure. This involves recognizing that failure is not a reflection of our worth as individuals, but rather a natural byproduct of taking risks and pursuing our goals. It requires us to let go of the need for external validation and to cultivate a sense of self-worth that is independent of external outcomes. Practicing self-compassion is essential on this journey. It means treating us with kindness and understanding, especially in moments of disappointment or self-doubt. By acknowledging our humanity and embracing our imperfections with warmth and acceptance, we can soften the blow of failure and create space for growth and healing to occur.

Learning to extract lessons from failure is also crucial. This involves reflecting on our experiences with curiosity and openness, rather than judgment or self-recrimination. It requires us to identify the factors that contributed to our failure and to discern the valuable insights that can be gleaned from our setbacks. By reframing failure as a teacher rather than a punishment, we can transform even the most painful experiences into opportunities for growth and self-improvement. Cultivating resilience is vital on this journey. It means bouncing back from failure with grace and determination, refusing to be defined by our setbacks or to allow them to derail our progress. It requires us to tap into our inner reserves of strength and perseverance, trusting in our ability to overcome obstacles and emerge stronger on the other side. Learning to embrace setbacks as steppingstones to success is perhaps the most challenging aspect of this journey. It involves relinquishing our attachment to the illusion of perfection and embracing the messy, imperfect nature of human experience. It requires us to trust in the wisdom of the journey, knowing that every setback brings us one step closer to our goals, and every failure is an opportunity to learn, grow, and ultimately, to succeed.

In the end, embracing setbacks is a journey of self-discovery and self-empowerment. It requires courage, resilience, and a willingness to confront the shadows that lurk within. Yet, with each setback we encounter and each failure we overcome, we reclaim a little more of our inner strength and resilience – untethered from the fear of failure and free to pursue our dreams with passion and determination.

26. Turning the Page: Moving On from Old Relationships

In the intricate tapestry of life, relationships are threading that weave through our experiences, shaping our identities and influencing our paths. But just as seasons change, so do relationships. Some endure the test of time, while others fade away like footprints in the sand. Moving on from old relationships is a crucial part of our personal growth journey—a process that requires courage, introspection, and a willingness to embrace the unknown.

Reflecting on the Past

Before embarking on the journey of moving on, it's essential to take a moment to reflect on the past. Reflecting doesn't mean dwelling on what could have been or drowning in regret; instead, it's about acknowledging the lessons learned and the memories shared. Every relationship, whether it ended on good or bad terms, leaves behind valuable insights that can help us navigate the future more wisely.

Acceptance and Forgiveness

The cornerstone of moving on is acceptance—acceptance of what was, what is, and what will be. It's about coming to terms with the fact that the relationship has run its course and that clinging onto the past only hinders our ability to move forward. Forgiveness, both of others and us, is a powerful tool in this process. By letting go of resentment and releasing ourselves from the burden of grudges, we free up space for healing and growth.

Redefining Self-Identity

Old relationships often become intertwined with our sense of self, making it challenging to separate who we are from who we were with that person. Moving on provides an opportunity to redefine our self-identity on our own terms. It's a chance to rediscover our passions, interests, and values outside the context of the past relationship. Embracing our individuality empowers us to chart a new course based on authenticity and self-awareness.

Cultivating Gratitude

Gratitude is a transformative force that can shift our perspective from loss to abundance. Instead of lamenting what we've lost, we can choose to focus on what we've gained from the experience. Every relationship, no matter how fleeting, leaves behind gifts in the form of memories, lessons, and personal growth. By cultivating gratitude for these gifts, we honor the past while opening ourselves up to the possibilities of the future.

Building a Support Network

Moving on from old relationships can feel like navigating uncharted waters, but we don't have to do it alone. Building a support network of friends, family, or even professional counselors can provide the encouragement and guidance we need to navigate this transition. Surrounding ourselves with people who uplift and empower us reminds us that we are not defined by our past relationships but by the strength of our connections with others.

Embracing the Journey Forward

Moving on from old relationships is not a linear process—it's a journey filled with twists, turns, and unexpected detours. Some days will be easier than others, and setbacks are inevitable. But with each step forward, we grow stronger, wiser, and more resilient. Embracing the journey forward means embracing the uncertainty of the future with an open heart and a steadfast belief in our ability to thrive, no matter what challenges may come our way.

In the grand tapestry of life, old relationships are but one thread among many. As we weave our way through the intricacies of love, loss, and growth, may we remember that each thread serves a purpose, no matter how brief or fleeting. And as we move on from old relationships, may we do so with grace, gratitude, and an unwavering commitment to writing the next chapter of our lives with courage and compassion.

Chronicles of the Heart:
Navigating the Tides of Time

Time is a vast ocean, offering both currents of opportunity and waves of challenge. Embrace its ebb and flow, for within its passage lies the opportunity to shape our stories.

27. The Twists of Time

Time, that enigmatic force, has a curious way of shaping our lives. It weaves through the fabric of existence, sometimes gently guiding us forward, while at other times, twisting and turning, leading us down unexpected paths. In this chapter, we explore how time can both amplify the negative and illuminate the positive aspects of our journey.

The Double-Edged Sword

Time, like a double-edged sword, holds the power to transform situations and relationships. Its passage can either enhance or erode the foundations of our experiences. A fleeting moment of joy can be immortalized in our memories, while a prolonged period of hardship can leave scars that linger long after the pain has faded. Understanding this duality is key to navigating the twists and turns that time inevitably brings.

Amplifying Challenges

In the crucible of time, challenges can intensify, casting shadows that seem insurmountable. What once appeared as minor obstacles may grow into formidable barriers, testing our resilience and resolve. Time can magnify our fears, doubts, and insecurities, creating a sense of stagnation or despair. Yet, it is often in these moments of darkness that the seeds of growth are sown, waiting patiently for the light of opportunity to shine through.

Unraveling Perspectives

As time unfolds, our perspectives shift and evolve, altering the way we perceive the world around us. What once seemed certain may become uncertain, and what appeared impossible may suddenly feel within reach. Time has a way of challenging our assumptions, forcing us to question our beliefs and values. It is through this process of introspection and reflection that we gain clarity and insight, allowing us to navigate the twists of time with greater understanding and purpose.

Resilience in Adversity

Despite the challenges that time may bring, it also has the remarkable ability to foster resilience and strength. In the face of adversity, we discover depths of courage and resilience we never knew existed within us. Time becomes a teacher, imparting valuable lessons in perseverance, adaptability, and grace under pressure. It is through overcoming obstacles that we emerge stronger, more resilient, and more capable of facing whatever the future may hold.

Seizing Opportunities

Just as time can amplify challenges, it can also illuminate opportunities, casting a light on new possibilities and pathways forward. What once seemed out of reach may suddenly become attainable, opening doors we never knew existed. Time invites us to embrace change, to seize the fleeting moments of opportunity that present themselves along the way. It is through embracing these opportunities that we unlock our full potential and embark on journeys of growth and self-discovery.

Embracing the Journey

In the grand tapestry of life, time is but a thread, weaving its way through the fabric of our experiences. It twists and turns, leading us down unexpected paths, but ultimately, it is up to us to navigate its twists and turns with courage and grace. By embracing the journey, both its challenges and its opportunities, we unlock the transformative power of time, harnessing its potential to shape our lives in ways we never thought possible.

28. Finding Strength in Being Alone

In a world that often celebrates companionship and connectivity, the concept of being alone can evoke a spectrum of emotions—fear, uncertainty, and even discomfort. However, solitude is not merely the absence of company but an opportunity for profound self-discovery and personal growth. In this chapter, we explore the transformative power of embracing solitude and finding strength in moments of aloneness.

The Paradox of Solitude

Solitude is often misunderstood as loneliness, yet they are distinct experiences. While loneliness stems from a sense of isolation or disconnection from others, solitude is a deliberate choice to be alone with oneself. It is within the stillness of solitude that we can hear the whispers of our own thoughts, explore the depths of our emotions, and connect with our innermost selves. Embracing solitude requires a shift in perspective, viewing it not as a void to be filled but as a space to be inhabited and explored.

Cultivating Self-Awareness

In the hustle and bustle of daily life, it's easy to lose sight of ourselves amidst the demands and expectations of others. Solitude offers a sanctuary for introspection and self-reflection, allowing us to tune into our own needs, desires, and values. By spending time alone, free from external influences, we can cultivate a deeper understanding of who we are and what truly matters to us. This self-awareness becomes the foundation upon which we build authentic connections with others and navigate life with clarity and purpose.

Nurturing Creativity and Inspiration

Solitude has long been associated with creativity and innovation, providing fertile ground for ideas to take root and flourish. When we're alone, our minds are free to wander, unconstrained by the distractions of the outside world. It is in these moments of quiet contemplation that inspiration strikes, leading to moments of insight and revelation. Whether through writing, art, or simply allowing our imagination to roam, solitude nurtures creativity and allows us to tap into the depths of our creativity.

Finding Inner Peace

In a world filled with noise and chaos, solitude offers a refuge for inner peace and tranquility. It is a sacred space where we can retreat from the pressures of life and recharge our spirits. Through practices such as meditation, mindfulness, or simply spending time in nature, we can cultivate a sense of calm and serenity within ourselves. In the stillness of solitude, we find solace, rejuvenating our minds, bodies, and souls.

Embracing the Journey Alone

Embracing solitude does not mean forsaking connections with others but rather honoring the relationship we have with ourselves. It is a journey of self-discovery and self-love, a path towards wholeness and authenticity. By embracing moments of aloneness, we reclaim our power and agency, becoming the authors of our own lives. Solitude becomes not a burden to bear but a gift to cherish—a sacred space where we can find strength, wisdom, and resilience in our journey through life.

29. Overcoming Anxiety with Resilience

In the labyrinth of the mind, anxiety lurks like a shadow, its tendrils reaching out to ensnare us in a web of fear and uncertainty. It manifests in the flutter of a racing heart, the knotting of a stomach, and the relentless chatter of worry that echoes through the corridors of our consciousness. Anxiety is not just a passing discomfort; it is an ever-present companion, casting a pall over even the brightest moments of our lives. Understanding anxiety requires peeling back the layers of its complexity, delving deep into the recesses of our psyche to uncover its roots. It may stem from past traumas, genetic predispositions, or the relentless pressure of modern life. Yet, regardless of its origins, anxiety takes hold with a tenacity that can feel suffocating, overwhelming us with its grip. In the midst of anxiety's storm, self-compassion becomes a beacon of light—a gentle reminder that we are not defined by our struggles. It is a call to treat ourselves with kindness and understanding, to offer ourselves the same grace that we would extend to a dear friend in need. Self-compassion is not about denying our pain or minimizing our suffering; rather, it is about holding space for ourselves with empathy and care, acknowledging our struggles while recognizing our inherent worth and dignity.

Mindfulness emerges as a lifeline in the tumult of anxiety, offering a sanctuary amidst the chaos of our thoughts and emotions. Through mindfulness practices such as meditation, deep breathing, or simply tuning into our senses, we can anchor ourselves in the present moment, finding refuge from the storm within. Mindfulness teaches us to observe our thoughts and sensations without judgment, allowing them to rise and fall like waves on the shore. In this space of non-reactive awareness, we cultivate a sense of calm and clarity that enables us to navigate the turbulent waters of anxiety with greater ease and resilience. Yet, even the most seasoned mariners cannot weather the storm alone. Seeking support from trusted allies—whether friends, family, or mental health professionals—can provide invaluable assistance on the journey towards healing. By reaching out for support, we acknowledge our vulnerability and strength in equal measure, forging connections that anchor us in times of need and uplift us in moments of despair. Building resilience becomes a beacon of hope in the darkness of anxiety—a reminder that we possess the strength and courage to weather life's storms. Resilience is not about avoiding difficult emotions or bypassing challenges; rather, it is about facing them head-on with courage and determination. It is about recognizing our capacity to bounce back from adversity, to learn and grow from our struggles, and to emerge from the depths of despair with newfound strength and wisdom.

In the crucible of anxiety, hope flickers like a flame, illuminating the path forward with its soft, steady glow. It is a reminder that, even in our darkest moments, we are not alone—that within the depths of our suffering lies the potential for growth, transformation, and healing. With each step forward, we reclaim our power and agency, forging a path towards a brighter, more resilient future—one anchored in compassion, mindfulness, and the unwavering belief that, even amidst the storm, there is always hope.

Finding Hope in the Darkness: While anxiety may cast a shadow over our lives, it does not have to define us. Within the darkness of anxiety lies the potential for growth, transformation, and healing. By acknowledging our struggles with honesty and vulnerability, we can begin to dismantle the barriers that anxiety erects around us and step into the light of hope and possibility. With each step forward, we reclaim our power and agency, forging a path towards a brighter, more resilient future.

Understanding Anxiety: Anxiety is more than just fleeting worry or nervousness; it is a pervasive and persistent feeling of unease that can interfere with daily life. It may stem from a variety of sources, including past traumas, genetic predispositions, or external stressors. Understanding the roots of our anxiety is the first step towards addressing it effectively. By identifying triggers and patterns, we can begin to unravel the tangled web of anxiety and reclaim control over our thoughts and emotions.

Embracing Mindfulness: Mindfulness is a powerful tool for managing anxiety, offering a refuge from the whirlwind of worries that often plague our minds. Through mindfulness practices such as meditation, deep breathing, or body scanning, we can anchor ourselves in the present moment, fostering a sense of calm and clarity. By observing our thoughts and sensations without judgment, we can break free from the cycle of anxious rumination and cultivate a greater sense of peace and serenity.

Seeking Support: Navigating anxiety alone can feel like trying to weather a storm without shelter. Seeking support from trusted friends, family members, or mental health professionals can provide invaluable assistance on the journey towards healing. Whether through therapy, support groups, or simply having a compassionate listener, reaching out for support can help us feel less alone in our struggles and empower us to face anxiety with courage and resilience.

Building Resilience: Resilience is the capacity to bounce back from adversity, and it is a quality that can be cultivated and strengthened over time. By developing healthy coping mechanisms, setting realistic goals, and practicing self-care, we can build our resilience muscles and become better equipped to face life's challenges, including anxiety. It's important to remember that resilience is not about avoiding difficult emotions but about facing them head-on with courage and determination.

Soul Whispers: Journeying into the Depths of Self

30. Loving Yourself as You Are

In the cacophony of voices that surround us—from social media influencers to societal expectations—it's easy to lose sight of our true selves. We're bombarded with messages telling us who we should be, how we should look, and what we should aspire to become. Yet, amidst this noise, there's a quiet, persistent whisper emanating from the depths of our souls—an invitation to embrace authenticity and love ourselves just as we are.

There was a time when I too found myself entangled in the web of external expectations and societal pressures. I chased after the elusive mirage of perfection, believing that my worthiness was contingent upon meeting impossible standards set by others. I compared myself relentlessly to those around me, measuring my worth by arbitrary metrics that left me feeling inadequate and unworthy. But amidst the noise and chaos of the outside world, there was a quiet, persistent voice within me—a whisper from the depths of my soul, urging me to embrace authenticity and love myself as I am. It was a journey fraught with challenges and setbacks, marked by moments of self-doubt and uncertainty. Yet, with each step forward, I discovered a newfound resilience within myself—a strength that allowed me to rise above the tide of negativity and embrace my true essence.

Through the practice of self-compassion, I learned to treat myself with kindness and understanding, offering myself the same warmth and empathy that I would extend to a cherished friend. I began to see my imperfections not as shortcomings to be hidden or fixed but as unique expressions of my humanity—symbols of my resilience and strength in the face of adversity. With time, I learned to unleash my inner authenticity, embracing my truth and living in alignment with my values and beliefs. I let go of the need for external validation, recognizing that my worthiness is inherent and unconditional. I stopped comparing myself to others, understanding that my journey is uniquely my own and that there is no one-size-fits-all definition of success or fulfillment. And as I journeyed deeper into the depths of self-discovery, I realized that my experience was not unique—those others, too, grappled with similar struggles and triumphs on their path to self-love and acceptance. I witnessed friends and loved ones navigating their own journeys of self-discovery, each forging their path with courage and resilience. Together, we shared stories of vulnerability and growth, offering each other support and encouragement along the way.

Today, as I reflect on my journey of self-discovery, I am filled with a profound sense of gratitude and awe for the person I have become. I have learned to love myself fiercely and unapologetically, embracing the messy, imperfect, beautifully flawed essence of who I am. And so can you, and so can we all. For within the depths of our beings lies an innate perfection—an inherent worthiness that transcends the fleeting judgments of the outside world. We are perfect as we are, each of us a unique expression of the divine, worthy of love, acceptance, and celebration.

31. A Journey through Depression

In the dimly lit corners of my mind, depression lurked like a specter, casting a shadow over every aspect of my existence. It was a weighty cloak that enveloped me, suffocating me with its tendrils of despair and hopelessness. In those dark moments, it felt as though I was drowning in a sea of sadness, unable to find my way back to the surface.

I know what it's like to wake up each day with a heavy heart, to feel as though the world is shrouded in darkness even when the sun is shining bright. I know what it's like to plaster on a smile and pretend that everything is okay, while inside, I'm crumbling under the weight of my own despair. I know what it's like to feel utterly alone, even in a room full of people, to wonder if anyone would notice if I disappeared entirely. But amidst the darkness, there was a glimmer of hope—a tiny spark that refused to be extinguished. It was the voice of resilience, whispering softly in the depths of my soul, urging me to keep going even when every fiber of my being screamed to give up. It was the knowledge that I was not alone—that there were others out there who understood my pain and stood ready to offer support and compassion. Through the haze of depression, I stumbled upon the path of self-discovery—a journey fraught with twists and turns, highs and lows. I learned to treat myself with kindness and compassion, to offer myself the same love and understanding that I would extend to a cherished friend. I discovered the power of therapy and medication, tools that helped me navigate the murky waters of my mind with greater clarity and purpose. Slowly but surely, I began to emerge from the shadows of depression, stepping into the light of self-acceptance and resilience. I learned to embrace my struggles as part of what made me who I am, to see them not as weaknesses to be ashamed of but as badges of honor, symbols of my strength and resilience in the face of adversity.

And though the journey was far from easy, it was a journey worth taking. For through the darkness of depression, I discovered a depth of compassion and empathy within myself that I never knew existed. I learned to appreciate the small moments of joy and beauty that punctuated the monotony of my daily life, to find solace in the simple act of breathing and being alive.

If you're reading this and you find yourself trapped in the grips of depression, know that you are not alone. There is hope, even in the darkest of moments, and there are people out there who care about you and want to help. Reach out, speak up, and know that brighter days lie ahead. You are stronger than you know, and you have the power to emerge from the shadows of depression and into the light of healing and wholeness.

32. Finding Light in Creative Expression

- **The Healing Power of Art**

Art has a remarkable ability to capture the essence of our emotions and experiences, giving voice to the unspoken and unseen. Whether through painting, drawing, or sculpting, art allows us to externalize our internal struggles, transforming them into tangible forms that we can see, touch, and interact with. In the process of creation, we find solace and catharsis, releasing pent-up emotions and finding clarity amidst the chaos of our minds.

- **The Therapeutic Rhythm of Music**

Music, with its melodic harmonies and rhythmic cadences, has a profound impact on our emotional well-being. It has the power to soothe our troubled souls, lifting us out of despair and carrying us to places of peace and tranquility. Whether through listening, playing, or composing, music provides a therapeutic outlet for our emotions, allowing us to connect with ourselves and others on a deeper level.

- ## **Dance: Movement as Medicine**

In the language of the body, dance becomes a form of liberation—a means of expressing emotions that words cannot adequately convey. Through movement, we release tension and stagnant energy, allowing it to flow freely through our bodies. Dance becomes a metaphor for our inner journey, a physical manifestation of the process of healing and transformation.

- ## **Writing: Unleashing the Power of Words**

Writing, in all its forms, offers a sanctuary for self-expression—a safe space where we can explore our thoughts, feelings, and experiences without fear of judgment or censure. Whether through journaling, poetry, or storytelling, writing allows us to give voice to our innermost thoughts and emotions, weaving them into narratives that reflect the complexity of the human condition.

- ## **Photography: Capturing Moments of Beauty**

In the lens of a camera, we find a tool for capturing moments of beauty and grace amidst the turmoil of life. Photography invites us to see the world through new eyes, to find meaning and purpose in the seemingly mundane. Through the act of framing and capturing images, we create a visual narrative of our experiences, preserving memories and moments that resonate with our souls.

- **Nature: Finding Solace in the Great Outdoors**

In the embrace of nature, we find solace and renewal—a reminder of our connection to something greater than ourselves. Whether through hiking, gardening, or simply spending time outdoors, nature provides a sanctuary for reflection and contemplation. It is in the stillness of the forest, the vastness of the ocean, and the majesty of the mountains that we find peace and perspective.

-In the tapestry of life, creative expression serves as a thread that binds us together—a common language that transcends barriers of language, culture, and circumstance. It is through art, music, dance, writing, photography, and nature that we find solace, healing, and connection in the midst of adversity. And though the journey may be fraught with challenges, we emerge stronger, more resilient, and more deeply connected to ourselves and the world around us.

Poems of Creative Healing

The eyes speak what the lips cannot articulate, conveying volumes of emotion in a single glance.

33. Palette of Emotions

In strokes of color bold and free,
I paint my soul's reality.
Each hue a whisper, each stroke a sigh,
Release the emotions I cannot deny.
With every brushstroke, I find release,
A moment of solace, a fleeting peace.
In the canvas of life, I create my art,
A reflection of the journey of my heart.

34. Melodies of Healing

In melodies sweet, I find my voice,
A symphony of healing, a timeless choice.
With each note played, I release the pain,
And find serenity in the music's refrain.
From minor chords to melodies bright,
I dance through the darkness into the light.
For in the rhythm of life, I find my song,
And with each note played, I grow strong.

35. Dance of Liberation

In the rhythm of my heartbeat,
I find freedom in movement sweet.
With every step, I release the chains,
And dance through the shadows, embracing the pains.
In the language of the body, I find my voice,
A dance of liberation, a reason to rejoice.
For in the movement of my feet, I find release,
And in the dance of life, I find my peace.

36. Words Unspoken

In the silence of the page, I find my voice,
A refuge for thoughts too heavy to voice.
With every word written, I release the pain,
And find solace in the stories I explain.
From prose to poetry, I weave my tale,
A journey of healing, a ship set to sail.
For in the power of words, I find my might,
And with each sentence penned, I find my light.

37. Captured Moments

In the lens of my camera, I find my truth,
A window to moments of beauty and youth.
With every click, I freeze time's embrace,
And find solace in the memories I trace.
From landscapes vast to faces dear,
I capture moments to hold them near.
For in the frame of the world, I find my art,
And with each picture taken, I heal my heart.

38. Eternal Embrace

In your embrace, I find my home,
Where I'm sheltered from the world's fierce roam.
Each touch a promise, each kiss a vow,
In your arms, I find solace now.
Beneath the moon's soft, silvery glow,
Our love blossoms, bright and aglow.
For in the dance of our hearts, I see, A timeless love, forever to be.

39. Unveiling the Soul

In the silence of my heart, I find the courage to be,
To embrace myself fully, wild and free.
For I am not defined by the standards of society,
But by the love that flows through me, a divine entity.
Each step I take is a dance of self-discovery,
As I unveil the layers of my soul with bravery.
For beneath the mask I wear for the world to see,
Lies the true essence of me, waiting to be set free.
In the depths of my being, I find the light,
A beacon of hope shining bright in the night.
For I am worthy of love, of joy, of grace,
And in loving myself, I find my rightful place.
So let me embrace myself with arms open wide,
And celebrate the beauty that lies inside.
For I am enough, just as I am,
A masterpiece of creation, a sacred lamb.

40. Embrace of Self

In the quiet of my soul, I find solace and peace,

As I journey within, seeking love's release.

For in the depths of my being, I find the key,

To unlocking the love that was always meant to be.

Each breath I take is a reminder of my worth,

A gentle whisper that echoes through the earth.

For I am enough, just as I am,

A masterpiece of creation, a radiant gem.

In the mirror's reflection, I see,

A warrior, a survivor, a soul wild and free.

For I've weathered the storms, conquered the pain,

And emerged stronger, ready to reclaim.

Each scar upon my skin is a testament,

To the battles fought and the victories won, heaven sent.

For they remind me of the strength within,

And the power of love to heal and mend.

So let me embrace myself, flaws and all,

For in loving myself, I stand tall.

For I am worthy of love, of joy, of peace,

And in loving myself, all my fears cease.

41. Petrichor's Poetry

Petrichor whispers tales of the earth,
As rain kisses the soil's rebirth.
A fragrance sweet, a scent divine,
A poetry written in nature's design.
With each rainfall, a verse is penned,
In the book of life, it will transcend.
In the essence of this aromatic domain,
I'm immersed in petrichor's poetry's reign.

42. Rhapsody of Rain

In the hush of night, when skies grow gray,
Rain tiptoes in, to have its say.
A silent messenger from realms unseen,
Bringing with it dreams unforeseen.
It starts as a whisper, a gentle patter,
Then crescendos into a rhythmic clatter.
Each drop a note in nature's symphony,
Crafting a tune of divine harmony.
The earth, a canvas, eagerly receives,
As rain paints landscapes with tender ease.
Leaves glisten, flowers bow in grace,
As rain weaves magic in every space.
In the city streets, it's a cleansing tide,
Washing away the dust, where dreams abide.
In rural lands, it's a lifeline bestowed,
Nurturing crops in its watery ode.
Oh, how the rain sings its rhapsody,
A melody of joy, of serenity.
In its gentle touch, we find release,
In the embrace of rain, we find peace.

43. The Journey Inward

In the depths of despair, where shadows loom,

There lies a path, through the heart's dark room.

A journey inward, where healing begins,

Where the soul finds solace, and the spirit wins.

Amidst the chaos, where storms rage wild,

There's a sanctuary within, where one finds a child.

A child of wonder, untouched by strife,

Yearning to reclaim the joy of life.

Step by step, in the labyrinth of the mind,

We navigate scars, both old and unkind.

Unraveling layers, shedding past pain,

Seeking the light, through the clouds of rain.

It's not a sprint, but a marathon long,

To heal from within, to emerge reborn.

With patience as our guide, and courage our shield,

We journey inward, to truths concealed.

Through whispered prayers and silent tears,

We confront our fears, release our fears.

We embrace our wounds, and let love in,

For healing begins from deep within.

In the chambers of the heart, where love resides,

We find the strength to let go of pride.

To forgive ourselves, and others too,

To mend what's broken, to start anew.
With each breath, we draw closer to peace,
As the scars of the past slowly cease.
In the stillness within, we find our grace,
And healing becomes a sacred embrace.
So let us journey inward, with open hearts,
And trust in the healing that inwardly starts.
For in the depths of our souls, lies the key,
To unlock the door to our truest destiny.

44. Unspoken Serenade

In the garden of the heart, love blooms,
A delicate flower, defying all dooms.
Its petals unfurl in shades of affection,
Binding souls in timeless connection.
Love is a melody, sweet and pure,
A symphony of emotions that endure.
It sings of joy in the brightest day,
And holds through darkness, come what may.
In the dance of love, hearts entwine,
Two souls merging in a cosmic design.
They weave a tapestry of hopes and dreams,
Navigating life's tumultuous streams.
Love is a journey, winding and vast,
A voyage of discovery, meant to last.
It leads us through valleys and mountain peaks,
Guiding us with the strength it seeks.
With love as our compass, we find our way,
Through the trials of night and the light of day.
It's the beacon that shines in the darkest hour,
A source of solace, a healing power.
So let us cherish love, in all its forms,
Embracing its beauty through life's storms.
For in its embrace, we find our true worth,

And experience the miracle of rebirth.
Love is the essence of our existence,
A force that defies all resistance.
In its eternal embrace, we find our home,
And know that we are never alone.

Summary

"You Are Incredibly Perfect" is a poignant collection of prose and poetry that delves deep into the day-to-day struggles and triumphs of human experience. Through beautifully crafted vignettes and heartfelt verses, the book explores themes of self-doubt, resilience, love, and growth etc. Each piece in the collection offers a glimpse into the lives of relatable characters navigating life's complexities. From the weight of expectations to the fleeting moments of joy, the book captures the full spectrum of emotions that accompany the journey of self-discovery. Through raw honesty and lyrical prose, the author invites readers to journey alongside the characters as they confront their inner demons, celebrate their victories, and find solace in the beauty of the ordinary. With each turn of the page, readers are reminded of the inherent imperfections that make us human and the inherent beauty in embracing them.

"You Are Incredibly Perfect" is a touching ode to the resilience of the human spirit and a gentle reminder that even in our darkest moments, we are worthy of love, acceptance, and belonging. It is a testament to the power of vulnerability and the transformative nature of embracing our flaws with grace and compassion.

A Final Note Of Thanks

As I reach the final pages of this book, I am filled with gratitude for the opportunity to share these words with you. Writing these chapters has been a journey of introspection, exploration, and growth, and I am deeply thankful for the privilege of accompanying you on your own journey. To you, dear reader, I extend my heartfelt thanks. Thank you for lending me your time and attention, for allowing my words to weave their way into the fabric of your thoughts and emotions. It is a profound honor to know that my words have resonated with you in some way, whether as a source of inspiration, solace, or encouragement. As you close this book and embark on the next chapter of your own story, I encourage you to carry its lessons with you – to embrace imperfection, to cultivate resilience, and to dare greatly in the pursuit of your dreams. Know that you are capable of overcoming any obstacle that stands in your way and that your journey is worthy of celebration, regardless of the twists and turns it may take. Remember, too, that you are never alone on this journey. Whether you find solace in the pages of a book, the embrace of a loved one, or the quiet whispers of your own heart, know that there is always supported to be found for those who seek it. As I bid you farewell, I offer these final words of gratitude and encouragement,

Thank you for sharing this journey with me. May your path be filled with light, love, and boundless possibility.

With deepest appreciation,

Avishka Singh

-,` ♡ ´-

Within the pages we've shared, may you find solace, wisdom, and delight, and may the journey through words continue to illuminate your path long after the last page is turned.